The Magic School Bus
Lost in the Solar System

By Joanna Cole / Illustrated by Bruce Degen

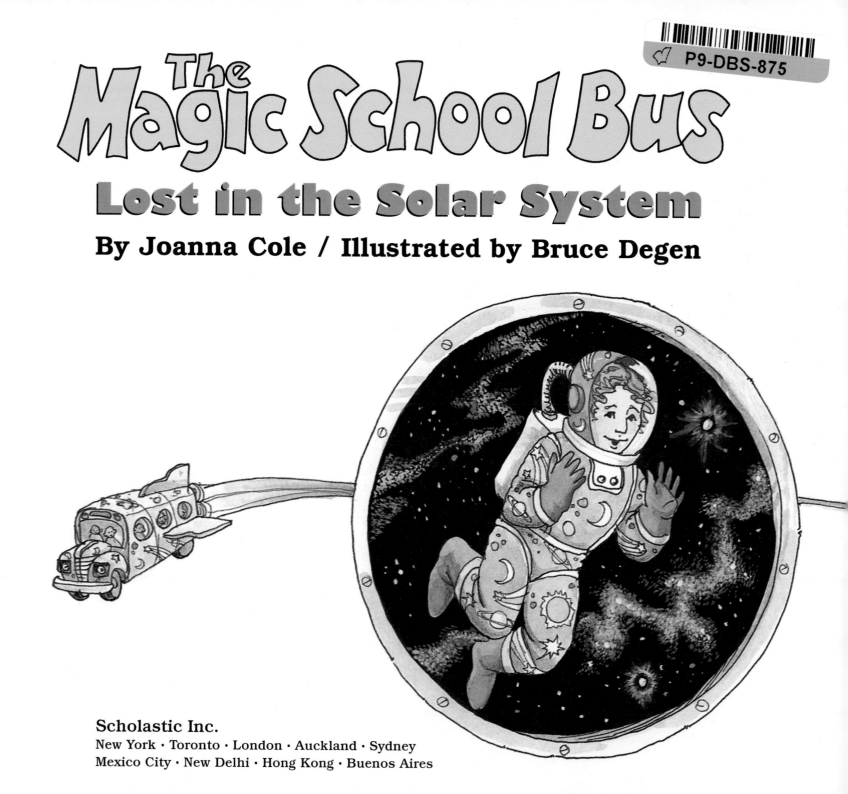

Scholastic Inc.

New York · Toronto · London · Auckland · Sydney
Mexico City · New Delhi · Hong Kong · Buenos Aires

The author and illustrator wish to thank Dr. Donna L. Gresh,
Center for Radar Astronomy at Stanford University,
for her assistance in preparing this book.

The author also thanks John Stoke, Astronomical Writer/Producer
at the American Museum-Hayden Planetarium, for his helpful advice,
and Dr. Ellis D. Miner, Cassini Science Manager, Jet Propulsion Laboratory,
for keeping us up-to-date with the latest astronomical measurements.

ISBN-13: 978-0-590-41429-6 / ISBN-10: 0-590-41429-1

42 41 40 39 38   14 15 16/0

Printed in the U.S.A.   40

The illustrator used pen and ink, watercolor,
color pencil, and gouache for the paintings in this book.

To Virginia and Bob McBride—J.C.

For Chris, queen of the
Biscadorian Mother ship—B.D.

WHAT IS THE SOLAR SYSTEM?
by John

The solar system is the Sun and all the bodies that orbit around it—the planets, their moons, the asteroids, comets, and other chunks of rock, ice and dust.

SUN

AL EINSTEIN
$E = mc^2$
MY FAVORITE THEORIST

ALFALFA
MY FAVORITE SPROUT

ORBIT

It was trip day again in Ms. Frizzle's class. Everyone was excited. We were going to the planetarium to see a sky show about the solar system.

CLASS, AN ORBIT IS THE PATH OF A PLANET OR OTHER OBJECT AROUND THE SUN.

Arnold's cousin Janet was
visiting our class for the day.
"I know all of you
will be nice to our guest," said the Friz.

5

We tried to be nice to Janet.
We really did.
As we got on the school bus,
we told her that Ms. Frizzle
is the weirdest teacher in school.
But Janet wasn't interested.
She wanted to tell us about herself.

MY SCHOOL IS TALLER THAN YOUR SCHOOL.

OUR SWINGS ARE BETTER THAN YOUR SWINGS.

MY TEACHER IS WEIRDER THAN YOUR TEACHER.

WHO WANTS A TALL SCHOOL?

As usual, it took a while to get the old bus started.
But finally we were on our way.
As we were driving, Ms. Frizzle told us all about how the Earth spins like a top as it moves in its orbit.
It was just a short drive to the planetarium, but Ms. Frizzle talked fast.

THIS BUS IS A WRECK.

AT LEAST IT STARTED THIS TIME.

WE HAVE NEW SCHOOL BUSES AT OUR SCHOOL.

WHAT MAKES NIGHT AND DAY?
    by Phoebe
The spinning of the Earth makes night and day.
    When one side of the Earth faces the Sun it is daytime on that side. When that side turns away from the Sun, it is night.

WHEN THE EARTH SPINS WE SAY IT ROTATES.
THE EARTH MAKES ONE ROTATION ~TURN~ EVERY DAY.

7

When we got to the planetarium,
it was closed for repairs.
"Class, this means we'll
have to return to school,"
said the Friz.
We were so disappointed!

On the way back,
as we were waiting at a red light,
something amazing happened.
The bus started tilting back,
and we heard the roar of rockets.
"Oh, dear," said Ms. Frizzle.
"We seem to be blasting off!"

Far behind, in the black sky, we saw the planet Earth getting smaller and smaller. We were traveling in space! We had become astronauts!

LOOK HOW SMALL THE EARTH SEEMS FROM HERE!

CLASS, NOTICE EARTH'S BLUE OCEANS, WHITE CLOUDS AND BROWN LAND.

IT'S BEAUTIFUL!

I THINK, I HAVE TO GO TO THE BATHROOM.

The Friz said our first stop
would be the Moon.
We got off the bus and looked around.
There was no air, no water,
no sign of life.
All we saw were dust and rock
and lots and lots of craters.
Ms. Frizzle said the craters were
formed billions of years ago
when the Moon was hit by meteorites.
Meteorites are falling chunks
of rock and metal.

WE ARE SO LIGHT ON THE MOON!

THAT'S BECAUSE THE MOON HAS LESS GRAVITY THAN THE EARTH.

YOUR WEIGHT AND FATE ON THE MOON

lbs.	lbs.
85	14
Earth Weight	Moon Weight

You will travel to far off places.

It was fun on the Moon.
We wanted to play,
but Ms. Frizzle said it was time to go.
So we got back on the bus.
"We'll start with the Sun,
the center of the solar system,"
said the Friz, and we blasted off.

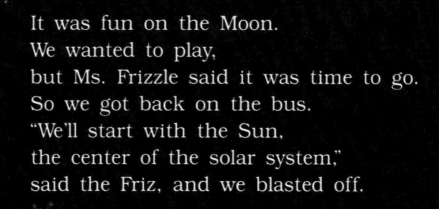

WHAT MAKES THE MOON SHINE?
by Rachel

The Moon does not make any light of its own. The moonlight we see from Earth is really light from the sun. It hits the Moon and bounces off, the way light is reflected from a mirror.

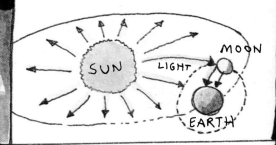

THE MOON'S ORBIT
by Amanda Jane

The Moon travels in orbit around the Earth, just as the Earth travels around the Sun.

13

THE SUN IS A STAR
by Carmen
Our Sun is an average star like the ones we see in the night sky.

WHICH STAR DO WE SEE ONLY IN THE DAYTIME?

THAT'S EASY: THE SUN.

HOW BIG IS THE SUN?
by Gregory
Our sun measures more than a million kilometers across. More than one million Earths could fit inside it!

We zoomed toward the Sun, the biggest, brightest, and hottest object in the solar system. Jets of super-hot gases shot out at us from the surface. Thank goodness Ms. Frizzle didn't get *too* close!

YOU SHOULD NEVER LOOK DIRECTLY AT THE SUN, CHILDREN. IT CAN DAMAGE YOUR EYES!

YOU SHOULD NEVER DRIVE A BUS DIRECTLY INTO THE SUN, EITHER!

HOT!

SOLAR FLARES are huge explosions on the Sun's surface.

She steered around to the other side
and pulled away.
"We'll be seeing all the planets
in order, class," explained Frizzie.
"Mercury is the first planet,
the closest to the Sun."

MY SCHOOL IS HEATED
WITH SOLAR ENERGY.

I HAVE A SUN DECK.

I HAVE TEN PAIRS
OF SUNGLASSES.

GIVE US A
BREAK, JANET.

HOW HOT IS THE SUN?
by Florrie
At the center of the sun
the temperature is about
15 million degrees Celsius!

The sun is so hot
it heats planets
that are millions
of kilometers away.

SUN SPOTS
are areas
that are cooler
than the rest
of the Sun.

Our Path So Far

Mercury was a dead, sun-baked planet.
"This planet is a lot like our Moon.
There is no water and hardly any air,"
said the Friz.
"Notice the craters on its surface
as we pass by."

THE SUN LOOKS SO MUCH BIGGER THAN IT DOES FROM EARTH.

THAT'S BECAUSE MERCURY IS SO CLOSE.

TOO CLOSE! LET'S GO!

YOUR WEIGHT AND FATE ON MERCURY

lbs. 85 Earth Weight	lbs. 32 Mercury Weight

You will Vacation in a Sunny spot.

Before long, we felt ourselves being pulled in by the gravity of Venus —the second planet from the Sun. Venus was completely covered by a thick layer of yellowish clouds. "We will now explore the surface of Venus," said Ms. Frizzle.

WHY ARE VENUS'S CLOUDS YELLOW?
by Tim
Earth's clouds are white because they are made of water vapor. Venus's clouds are made mostly of a deadly yellow poison called sulfuric acid.

WE'RE GAINING WEIGHT, AND WE HAVEN'T EVEN HAD LUNCH.

WE WILL BE HEAVIER HERE THAN ON THE MOON OR MERCURY BECAUSE VENUS HAS MORE GRAVITY.

YOUR WEIGHT AND FATE ON VENUS

lbs.	lbs
85	77
Earth Weight	Venus weight

Your future looks cloudy.

SO DOES VENUS!

WHY IS IT SO HOT ON VENUS?
by Ralph
Venus's atmosphere has a lot of carbon dioxide gas in it. Carbon dioxide acts like a blanket to hold heat in.

CLOUDS
HEAT HEAT HEAT

When heat is trapped like this by a planet's atmosphere, it is called the "greenhouse effect."

Below the clouds, Venus was as dry as a desert.
The ground was covered with rocks.
And it was HOT!
It was about 460 degrees Celsius!
That's *much* hotter than an oven baking cookies!

THERE'S NO LIFE ON VENUS, CLASS.

IT'S TOO HOT!

IT'S TOO DRY!

THERE'S TOO MUCH ACID!

LET'S LEAVE!

The air was so heavy
we could feel it pressing down on us!
Ms. Frizzle said there might be active volcanoes
around, too.
We said, "Let's get out of here!"
"Our next stop is Mars,
the red planet, fourth from the Sun,"
announced the Friz.
"On our way, we'll be passing through
the orbit of Earth, the third planet."
The bus lifted off with a roar.

IT NEVER RAINS ON VENUS
by Dorothy Ann
Venus's clouds never make rain because it is too hot for rain to form. Any liquid on Venus dries up instantly.

I'VE BEEN TO MARS LOTS OF TIMES.

JUST IGNORE HER.

Our Path So Far

Looking down, we saw a huge canyon.
Ms. Frizzle said it was
as long as the United States.
There was a volcano
three times taller than
the tallest volcano on Earth.
And all around, there were channels
that looked like dried-up riverbeds.
Ice can be found under the soil.

Is THERE LIFE ON MARS?
by Molly
No life has been
found on Mars.
Living things need
water, and there
is no liquid water
on Mars.
So space scientists
think life probably
cannot exist there!

Polar Ice Cap

Canyon

Channels

YOUR WEIGHT AND FATE ON MARS

lbs. 85 Earth Weight	lbs. 32 Mars Weight

EARTH IS THE
BEST PLANET FOR
LIFE. THAT'S WHY
I LIVE THERE.

Things will
look rosy
soon.

JANET LIKES TO
BE THE BEST.

WE NOTICED.

"Mars is the last of what we call the inner planets!" Ms. Frizzle shouted above the roar of the rockets. "We will now be going through the asteroid belt to the outer planets!"

THE ASTEROID BELT
by Shirley

The area between the inner and the outer planets is called the asteroid belt. It is filled with thousands and thousands of asteroids.

WHAT ARE ASTEROIDS?
by Florrie

Asteroids are chunks of rock and metal in orbit around the sun.

They may be building blocks of a planet that never formed. Or they could be pieces of planets that broke apart.

Thousands of asteroids were spinning all around us.
All at once, we heard the tinkling of broken glass.
One of our taillights had been hit by an asteroid.
Ms. Frizzle put the bus on autopilot and went out to take a look.
She kept on talking about asteroids over the bus radio.

THE LARGEST ASTEROID IS ONLY 1/3 THE SIZE OF OUR MOON. MOST ASTEROIDS ARE THE SIZE OF HOUSES OR SMALLER.

I WISH SHE'D COME INSIDE.

Suddenly there was a snap.
Ms. Frizzle's tether line had broken!
Without warning,
the rockets fired up,
and the bus zoomed away!
The autopilot was malfunctioning.

On the radio, Ms. Frizzle's voice grew
fainter and fainter.
Then she was gone.
We were on our own!
We were lost in the solar system!

KIDS, I'LL MEET YOU LATER... LATER... LATER

COME IN, MS. FRIZZLE. DO YOU READ ME?

Most of us were too scared to move.
But Janet started searching the bus.
In the glove compartment
she found Ms. Frizzle's lesson book.
As she began reading from it,
a huge planet came into view.
"Class, this is Jupiter," Janet read.
"It's the first of the outer planets,
and the largest planet in the solar system."

"As we approach Jupiter, we can see some of its many moons."

"Arnold, are you listening?"

BOY, MS. FRIZZLE PLANS EVERYTHING!

SHE SHOULDN'T TOUCH MS. FRIZZLE'S THINGS.

BUT THIS IS AN EMERGENCY!

Lesson Plan
As we approach Jupiter, we can see some of its many moons.
"Arnold, are you ...?"

WHAT ARE SATURN'S RINGS?
by Rachel

Saturn's rings are made of ice, rock and dust — all in orbit around the planet.

The next sight made us forget our troubles.
It was Saturn, a gas planet like Jupiter.
It had swirling clouds and lots of moons.
But the most incredible thing about Saturn
was its rings.
It was the most beautiful planet
in the solar system!

YOUR WEIGHT AND FATE ON SATURN

lbs.	lbs.
85	91
Earth Weight	Saturn Weight

There's a ring in your future.

"There are thousands of rings around Saturn, class."

THEY LOOK LIKE THE GROOVES IN AN OLD PHONOGRAPH RECORD.

SATURN IS THE GROOVIEST PLANET, MAN!

28

THE TIPPED OVER PLANET
by Ralph
Uranus spins differently from the other planets. It seems to be lying on its side compared to most other planets in the Solar system.

Uranus   Earth   Sun

YOUR WEIGHT AND FATE ON URANUS

lbs. 85 Earth Weight   lbs. 77 Uranus Weight

Feeling blue? You may be homesick.

Next was Uranus, a blue-green gas planet with faint gray rings and moons. Some scientists think they might be made of chunks of graphite— the material used in pencils on Earth.

"Methane gas in its atmosphere makes Uranus look blue."

YOU LOOK KIND OF BLUE YOURSELF.

I'M FREEZING!

THAT'S BECAUSE WE'RE SO FAR AWAY FROM THE SUN.

The bus was going faster and faster,
and we couldn't control the autopilot.
We swept past stormy Neptune,
another blue-green planet—eighth from the Sun.
All we could think about
was finding Ms. Frizzle!

"Neptune
is the last
of the giant
gas planets."

WE'RE ALMOST
OUT OF GAS
OURSELVES!

AND THE NEAREST
SERVICE STATION
IS 4,000 MILLION
KILOMETERS AWAY.

HOW LONG IS A YEAR?
by Tim
A year is the time
it takes for a planet
to go all around the
sun. Neptune and
Uranus are so far away
from the sun that
they have very long
years.
One year on Uranus is
84 Earth years.
Neptune's year is
165 Earth years.

YOUR WEIGHT AND FATE
ON NEPTUNE

lbs.
85
Earth
Weight

lbs.
97
Neptune
Weight

You will have a
happy birthday
165 years from now.

IS PLUTO A REAL PLANET?
by Wanda

People used to call Pluto a planet. Then scientists saw a lot of small bodies out beyond Pluto. They are called "Kuiper Belt Objects" — KBOs for short.
Now scientists call Pluto a KBO, or plutoid.

We were going so fast,
we almost missed seeing Pluto
and its moons.
Charon is the biggest one,
and Hydra and Nix are smaller.
We were so far away from the sun
that it didn't look big anymore.
It just looked like a very, very bright star.

YOUR WEIGHT AND FATE ON PLUTO

lbs.	lbs.
85	6
Earth Weight	Pluto Weight

You will meet a small, dark plutoid.

I DON'T SEE ANYTHING BUT STARS.

ANOTHER STAR MAY HAVE LIFE ON ONE OF ITS PLANETS.

WE'LL HAVE TO WAIT AND SEE.

I HOPE MS. FRIZZLE IS WAITING, TOO.

CHARON

PLUTO

Janet flipped rapidly
through Ms. Frizzle's book.
Suddenly she found something new—
the instructions for the autopilot.
We punched in ASTEROID BELT
on the control panel.
Slowly the bus turned around.
It was working! We were going back!

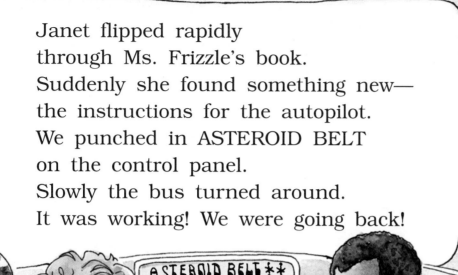

JANET REALLY SAVED THE DAY.

I TOLD YOU SHE'S A GOOD KID.

Our Path so far

Asteroid Belt

When we reached the asteroid belt, there was Ms. Frizzle!

HEY, THAT ASTEROID IS DRESSED FUNNY.

THAT'S NOT AN ASTEROID, IT'S MS. FRIZZLE!

BOY, AM I GLAD TO SEE HER.

ME TOO!

With Frizzie back at the wheel,
the bus headed straight for Earth.
We reentered the atmosphere,
landed with a thump,
and looked around.

We were in the school parking lot again.
The rockets were gone.
The space suits were gone.
The bus was a wreck.
Everything was back to normal.

OUR PLANET CHART

PLANET	HOW BIG ACROSS	HOW LONG ONE ROTATION	HOW LONG ONE YEAR	HOW FAR FROM THE SUN (AVERAGE)	HOW MANY KNOWN MOONS	ARE THERE RINGS?
MERCURY	4,878 km.	58.6 days	88.0 Earth days	57.9 million km.	None	No
VENUS	12,104 km.	243.0 days	224.7 Earth days	108.2 million km.	None	No
EARTH	12,756 km.	23.9 hours	365.3 Earth days	149.6 million km.	1	No
MARS	6,794 km.	24.6 hours	687.0 Earth days	227.9 million km.	2	No
JUPITER	142,984 km.	9.9 hours	11.9 Earth years	778.3 million km.	63	Yes
SATURN	120,536 km.	10.7 hours	29.5 Earth years	1,429.4 million km.	46	Yes
URANUS	51,118 km.	17.2 hours	84.0 Earth years	2,871.0 million km.	27	Yes
NEPTUNE	49,528 km.	16.1 hours	164.8 Earth Years	4,504.3 million km.	13	Yes

In the classroom,
we made a terrific
chart of the planets
and a mobile of the solar system.

OUR SOLAR SYSTEM

Neptune

⑥Saturn

Asteroid Belt

③Earth

①Mercury

Sun

②Venus

④Mars

⑤Jupiter

⑦Uranus

YOUR WEIGHT AND FINE ON EARTH

lbs.
85
Earth Weight

HOW ABOUT THAT? I WEIGH 85 POUNDS.

There's no place like home.

At last, it was time to go home.
It had been a typical day
in Ms. Frizzle's class.
Now we had only one problem.
Would anyone ever believe us
when we told about our trip?

OUR FISH FRIENDS

OCEANS & SEAS

ATTENTION, READERS!

DO NOT ATTEMPT THIS TRIP ON YOUR OWN SCHOOL BUS!

Three reasons why not:

1. Attaching rockets to your school bus will upset your teacher, the school principal, and your parents. It will not get you into orbit anyway. An ordinary bus cannot travel in outer space, and you cannot become astronauts without years of training.

2. Landing on certain planets may be dangerous to your health. Even astronauts cannot visit Venus (it's too hot), Mercury (it's too close to the Sun), or Jupiter (its gravity would crush human beings). People cannot fly to the Sun, either. Its gravity and heat would be too strong.

3. Space travel could make you miss dinner with your family... for the rest of your childhood. Even if a school bus could go to outer space, it could never travel through the entire solar system in one day. It took years for the Voyager space probes to do that.

ON THE OTHER HAND...

If a red-haired teacher in a funny dress shows up at your school — start packing!